Dr. Hilda
Makes House Calls

By Mabel Watts
Illustrated by Steven Petruccio

A GOLDEN BOOK • NEW YORK
Western Publishing Company, Inc., Racine, Wisconsin 53404

Just as Dr. Hilda and Marigold were leaving
to go on a picnic with a basket full of
sandwiches, carrot sticks, cupcakes, and
apple juice, the telephone rang.

"Hello," said Dr. Hilda. "What can I do
for you?"

It was Jenny James, and she could hardly
speak for crying.

"Sam, my cat, is sick," she said. "He will not eat, and he will not play. All he does is meow! Can you please come quick?"

"We were going on a picnic," said Dr. Hilda, "but we can't do that with your cat so sick. We'll come right over."

"Yes, we'll go and help," said Marigold. "Our picnic can wait."

And away they went on their big red motorcycle. Dr. Hilda was in front, and Marigold held on tight to her back. With the doctor's first-aid bag strapped on behind, full of pills and potions and a lot of get-well things, they zoomed along.

Soon they arrived at Jenny's house. Sam the cat didn't look very well. "He isn't his usual self," said Jenny. "Everything hurts but his whiskers and his tail."

"We'll fix that," said Dr. Hilda. She picked up Sam by the scruff of his neck. "You have flea bites all over," she said. "And the more you scratch, the more holes you will make in your fur."

Dr. Hilda popped a pill into Sam's mouth to calm him down. Then she covered his bites with a healing ointment and fastened a flea collar around his neck so the fleas would go away.

"Now your cat will get well," said Dr. Hilda.

"Oh, thank you," said Jenny. "Thank you very much." Sam the cat meowed a big meow.

Then away sped Dr. Hilda and Marigold on their big red motorcycle.

"Now we can go on our picnic," said Marigold.

But when they got home, they found that someone had left a note. "Dear Dr. Hilda," it said, "Danny, my dog, has a terrible toothache. Will you please come and help? Signed, Alfred."

"Our picnic will have to wait," Dr. Hilda told Marigold.

"We can't leave Alfred's dog with a terrible toothache," said Marigold.

And off they went, Dr. Hilda and Marigold, on their big red motorcycle—chug-a-lug, chug-a-lug—to Alfred's house.

Alfred had red hair and freckles, and so did Danny, his dog. "Danny is just like a brother," Alfred said. "When he hurts, I hurt, too."

Marigold held Danny's paw and patted the top of his head. "Don't worry, Danny. Dr. Hilda will make the hurt go away," she said.

While Dr. Hilda hunted through the first-aid bag, Marigold kept patting the top of Danny's head so he would know someone cared. Then Dr. Hilda pulled the aching tooth.

Right away Danny felt a whole lot better. He wagged his tail and barked his thanks.

"Hurray!" said Marigold. "Now we can go on our picnic!"

But that was not to be...not yet. The
moment Dr. Hilda and Marigold got
home, they found a carrier pigeon trying to
deliver a message. When the pigeon saw
Dr. Hilda chugging to a stop, it dropped a
letter on the front lawn.

"Dear Dr. Hilda," said the letter,
"Tony, my pony, jumped over a prickly
hedge and got some prickles in his hoof.
Will you please come and get them out?
Signed, Tom."

"We could never enjoy our picnic if we didn't go and help," said Marigold.

So, once again, away Dr. Hilda and Marigold went on their motorcycle with a *brruumm, brruumm,* and with the doctor's first-aid bag strapped on the back and the wind whistling by.

They came to a stable where Tom was waiting with Tony. Tony was doing a lot of neighing because he was hurting a lot.

Dr. Hilda examined Tony's sore hoof while Marigold patted his head. "No more clippety-clop until the doctor gets the prickles out," Marigold told Tony.

Dr. Hilda got the prickles out, and Tony said thank you in his ponyish way. Then, with a little help from Tom, Dr. Hilda bathed the sore hoof and put an extra-large bandage over the wound.

"Thank you, Dr. Hilda. Thank you very much," said Tom.

Then away went Dr. Hilda and
Marigold on their big red motorcycle. And
do you know what they did? They went on
their picnic—at last!

In the woods, under an oak tree, they ate
their sandwiches, carrot sticks, and
cupcakes and drank their apple juice. They
fed the squirrels, and they watched the
rabbits. And they talked about how happy
they were to have helped so many animals,
all on their picnic day.